THE JELLYBEANS
and the Big Dance

BY LAURA NUMEROFF AND NATE EVANS

ILLUSTRATED BY LYNN MUNSINGER

Abrams Books for Young Readers, New York

The illustrations in this book were made with
watercolor on paper.

Library of Congress Cataloging-in-Publication Data:

Numeroff, Laura Joffe.
The Jellybeans and the big dance / Laura Numeroff.
p. cm.
Summary: When four young girls meet in dance class, it takes time for them to find
a way—and a reason—to pull together as one, but Emily helps them realize that,
just like a bag of jellybeans, they can be different and still go well together.
ISBN 978-0-8109-9352-5 (hcj)
[1. Dance—Fiction. 2. Dance recitals—Fiction. 3. Animals—Fiction.] I. Title.

PZ7.N964Jel 2007
[E]—dc22
2006031983

Text copyright © 2008 Laura Numeroff and Nate Evans
Illustrations copyright © 2008 Lynn Munsinger

Book design by Chad W. Beckerman

Printed and bound in U.S.A.
10 9 8 7 6 5 4 3 2

harry n. abrams, inc.
a subsidiary of La Martinière Groupe

115 West 18th Street
New York, NY 10011
www.hnabooks.com

Emily loved to dance.

She danced while waiting
for the school bus,

she danced while
watching TV,

and she even danced while
brushing her teeth.

Emily skipped all the way to her first dance class. She walked into the studio and looked around. She saw one girl reading a book, one playing with a soccer ball, and one drawing in a sketchbook.

"Welcome," the teacher said. "I'm Miss Tingly-Weezer.
Please put your things in the cubbies."

Emily saw name tags on the cubbies:
Emily, Nicole, Bitsy, and Anna.

The girl playing with the ball shoved it into the one marked "Nicole."

"I love to dance," said Emily.

"Not me," Nicole said. "I like to play soccer. My mom made me take this class."

"I'd rather paint," said Bitsy.

Anna shyly put her book away.

"In a month we will have a recital," Miss Tingly-Weezer said. "We will be dancing to a delightful song called 'Oh, Little Bug!'"

"Bugs are icky," said Bitsy.

"I'm afraid of bugs," Anna mumbled.

"My little brother ate a bug once!" Nicole shared.

Emily was disappointed. She was hoping to be something wonderful, like a princess, not a bug. And it looked like she wasn't going to be friends with Anna, Nicole, and Bitsy, either. They had nothing in common.

Miss Tingly-Weezer had them make a circle
and spin around and around.

Bitsy got dizzy and bumped into Emily, who knocked into the cubbies. Their name tags fell onto the floor.

"Hey," said Emily, "the first letters of our names spell BEAN!"

"I hate beans," said Nicole.

The next few classes were just as awful. After the fourth one, Emily got into the car with her mother.

"Our dance should be called 'The No-Good Bugs,'" Emily grumbled. She was very disappointed with her new dance class.

"Would a trip to Petunia's cheer you up?" her mother asked.

"Yippee!" said Emily.

Emily looked over all the candy. She finally decided on something special that she hoped would make dance class better.

The next day, Emily twirled and jumped

while the other girls fumbled their steps.

After class, Emily asked, "Remember how our names spell out 'BEAN'?"

Emily gave each girl a little bag. They opened them quickly.

"Jellybeans! I love jellybeans," said Bitsy.

"Me, too!" said Nicole.

"They're my favorite candy," said Anna, jumping up and down.

"Jellybeans are all different flavors, but they still go well together," said Emily. "Maybe we could, too. We can be the dancing Jellybeans!"

Everyone liked that idea.

"But our dance is still about icky bugs," Bitsy complained.

"I bet we can figure out a way to make this recital really great!" said Emily.

Anna showed them books about bugs at the library.
They found some bugs they actually thought were cute!

Bitsy helped the girls design their costumes.

Nicole taught them exercises she learned from soccer to get them in shape.

And Emily worked with the others on their dance steps.

Finally the big night arrived.

"Ladies and gentlemen . . . I proudly present . . . the Jellybeans!" Miss Tingly-Weezer announced. "They will now perform 'Oh, Little Bug!'"

The Jellybeans took their places onstage.

Emily looked at the audience. She had never seen so many people in one place. Miss Tingly-Weezer began playing the piano. All of a sudden, Emily realized she didn't remember any of the steps.

"What's wrong?" Nicole whispered.

"I'm scared!" said Emily.

Nicole took Emily's hand and started to do some silly
soccer kicks. Then Anna and Bitsy started kicking, too.

Emily was having so much fun that she forgot
to be scared and remembered her steps.

The Jellybeans did "Oh, Little Bug!" from beginning to end. They twirled and skipped. They tiptoed and jumped. They danced and pranced and boogie-woogied.

The crowd whistled and clapped. "Hooray for the Jellybeans!" they cheered. The Jellybeans bowed, and then went backstage to change.

Presenting
The
Jellybeans
in
"Oh, Little
Bug!

"I almost messed up the recital," Emily said.

"But it was perfect!" said Anna.

"Your kicks were great!" said Nicole. "I bet you'd be good at soccer."

"We could be the Jellybean Soccer All-Stars!" Bitsy said.

"I just hope I don't forget when to kick," Emily said.

Then they all went to Petunia's for their favorite candy . . .

JELLYBEANS!